Fabius Maximus Ray

The Christmas Tree and Other Poems

Fabius Maximus Ray

The Christmas Tree and Other Poems

ISBN/EAN: 9783337379667

Printed in Europe, USA, Canada, Australia, Japan

Cover: Foto ©Andreas Hilbeck / pixelio.de

More available books at **www.hansebooks.com**

THE

CHRISTMAS TREE,

AND

OTHER POEMS,

BY

F. M. RAY.

PORTLAND, ME.:

DRESSER, McLELLAN & CO.,

47 EXCHANGE STREET,

1874.

To ALBERT B. OTIS, ESQUIRE,

OF BOSTON, MASS.,

In fulfilment of a promise made in school days, (with far more seriousness, however, than was to be confessed at the time,) this little volume is affectionately inscribed by his sincere friend,

THE AUTHOR.

CONTENTS.

CONTENTS.

THE CHRISTMAS TREE.

The Christmas Tree.

I.

CHRISTMAS EVE.

The stars are bright in the wintry sky,
And the wind is cold, oh, piercing cold !
But the Christmas bells chime merrily
Up in the belfry brown and old.

And cheerily on the high church walls,
From vaulted roof to nave below,
A brilliant light from the gasjets falls
And fills the room with a midday glow.

Anon, with bright and beaming eyes,
The rosy children crowd the aisles,
And quick expectant pleasure flies
To wreathe each dimpled mouth with smiles.

For wondrous sights they soon have seen
Which fill their childish hearts with glee,
Amid the branches, emerald green,
Of yonder heavy laden tree.

And little lips have lisped, no doubt,
"On earth peace, good will toward men ;"
Perchance have guessed the meaning out
So oft obscured to older ken.

No cares to vex, their hearts are light
In parents' constant love secure ;
Their eyes are bright with true delight,
For Santa Claus is coming sure.

True innocence maketh all hearts light ;
But innocent eyes look strange and wild ;
And they are the eyes surpassingly bright
Of that little waif, the beggar child,

Who hath climbed a fence in the wintry air,
And is looking in at a window high,
While a child within, who sees her there,
Is asking its mother if angels are nigh.

II.

THE BEGGAR GIRL.

Through many and many a weary day
She'd begged her bread from door to door ;
But her childish heart had kept at bay
The cares that prey on the grown-up poor.

And clad in rags that the wind blew through
She'd trod, thin shod, on pavements stark,
And naught of home or luxury knew,
Except from glances stolen through
The windows bright, when the nights were
    dark.

III.

THE LOVERS.

A youth high born and the village belle
To-morrow will wed,—on Christmas day :
A courtship brief, but they love full well,—
"A heaven-made match," says the *beau-monde*
    gay.

High hopes are lavished, and prodigal gold,
On the millionnaire's luxurious son ;
But lips now hushed in the church-yard mould
Will never more tell of the wrongs he hath
    done :

At least to the world that tenderly deals
With the sins of a man because they are human,
But the holiest horror instinctively feels
For his fellow sinner, too credulous woman !

Oh Christian folk who on Christmas eve
In the book of life your good deeds write,
Must not the Pharisees sorely grieve
The Lord who loveth the true and right?

The Lord of the just, whose natal morn
The joyous bells are ringing in ;—
Mild Mary's son, in manger born,
Who loved the world though lost in sin.

IV.

THE WEDDING.

Again his round hath Phœbus gone,
And wedding bells were rung to-day ;
Two hearts were joined, two souls made one
By words we heard the Rector say.

Fair orange flowers in the bride's bright hair
May have startled a conscience now and then ;
But the bridegroom thought they were right-
        fully there,
And esteemed himself most happy of men.

But when they came out from the high church
        door,
A little girl in her tattered gown

Was standing near by, and ran before,
As the crowd fell back to let them pass down.

And some there were about the door
Who marked that her eyes and mouth were
    the same
As the man's who rode with his coach and four,
Resembling his mother, a stately dame.

And that stately dame herself that day,
When the beggar girl looked up and smiled
At the wedding guests, as they rode away,
Wondered where else she had seen the child.

For a single glance at that little brown face
Her memory puzzled almost to pain ;
But the thread of the mystery she ne'er could
    trace,
Although she essayed it again and again.

And although her pride would have scorned
    the thought
That the being in rags was her own proud
    blood,
She sent her footman and had her brought
To be clothed with new clothes and fed with
    good food.

For a kindly spot is in every heart,—
Whether by sinner or saint possessed,
And high and low must bear their part
To lighten the cares of those distressed.

And surely gospel truths if strown
By the winds of chance in fallow souls,
The Lord will never refuse to own
Who, by constant laws, e'en chance controls.

So we will hope that our new-wed pair
May many a merry Christmas see,
And children's children with them share
The love that blooms on the Christmas tree.

For we ne'er may right a social wrong
By waste of breath or weak complaining,
Or humble the proud and subdue the strong
By more than mortal goodness feigning.

There's an eastern adage reflects our faith,
And I trust for profit will never fail,
As its words of wisdom it tersely saith :
"The truth is mighty and will prevail."

CASTE.

Beauteous mermaiden.
　　Child of the emerald sea!
Comest with pearls laden
　　Forth from the surging sea :
Glisten in thy dripping locks
　　Myriad salt-beads, crystalline :
Like a vision of love thou risest
　　Forth from the ocean green.

Tell me, oh mermaid, where is thy home ?
　For the ocean is deep and extendeth far,
And years o'er its breast the sailor may roam,
　Till his locks are white as the wave-crests are.

"Look, oh poet, out over the sea
　"Where those lone rocks pierce the tide,
"Lashed by the billows incessantly,
"Which rise and fall on the ocean wide.
"Deep, deep at the foot of that treacherous ledge,
　"In the hulk of a wreck is the merman's home.
"When the wind is still, to the water's edge
　The masts of the shipwrecked vessel come :
"And the pennon that once in the proud breeze
　　　rode,
　"Telling her name to the passing day,
"Now marks the mariner's last abode,
　"Ten fathoms in water long left to decay!

"The merman old, many children hath he,
"And is proud of us all as parent can be;
"And all are wedded, well wedded, but me.
    "But I, unfortunate, ventured to love
"Where love could ne'er requited be:
    "Madly I ventured to look above
"My kith and kindred of the sea:
        "And now I'm doomed to a lonely life
        "Who might have been a merman's wife!"

Once, dear reader, in the leafy June,
When the song-bird sings his sweetest tune,
    To the sea-side a pale painter came,—
    Save that on his cheek a spot like flame
And his own madders glowed each afternoon.
    The morning he was pale as death.
And a dry cough told how soon
    Must cease his feeble breath:
But in his deep dark eye that brighter grew
As nearer to a close his frail life drew,
    Were wealth of soul and gentleness of heart,
    Making his lips with a holy smile to part.
Each morn he spread his palette with the hues
That nature wore when fresh with early dews:
    And on the hill-side near a lovely cove,
Backgrounded by a woodland green,
    Till sultry noon, unceasingly he strove
To animate his canvas with the scene.

But when the sun was in his midday glow,
  Beneath a goodly maple's mellow shade
Would our wan and weary painter go,
  Where of the boughs and moss some hand
    had made
A rustic seat alluring him to rest.
There, from a pocket 'neath his vest,
  He'd take a much worn book and read.
Giving it an hour of undivided heed.
But when he had restored it to its wonted place,
And a smile of holy joy lit up his face,
  He remembered aught more precious still,
  And suddenly with tears his eyes would fill.
And the mermaid under the summer sea.
To whom all human things were mystery,
  Knew not it was a simple picture case
  Wherein only the limner light did trace
  The semblance of a stately woman's face,
Relieved by flaxen tresses, beauteous and soft.
Around a head by pride just raised aloft.
  The mermaid saw with tender sympathy,
  From her lurking place beneath the sea.
How his eyes brimmed o'er with tears,
  Responsive to his nameless grief,
  Till his soul yielded to their sweet relief,—
For mercy's angels are those holy tears!—
  But though her sorrows were than his more
    deep,

The little mermaid never dared to weep;
For by the laws of merman life, who weeps
          must die!
And with that soulless race there is no life on high.

Till autumn came, the painter wrought and read,
And with his life, his hopeless sorrow fed;
     But when his work was well nigh done,
And the forest's first ripe leaves were red,
     And toward the winter solstice sank the sun,
The painter weaker grew and died.
     And there was made for him a grave
Close by the ever surging ocean's side,
     And his requiem sang the tuneful wave!

Oh, unnatural and remorseless Fate!
Requiting love with neglect,—better hate,—
     Oh, unnatural tie, when virtue is allied
     By love, to aught so base as Pride!
The likeness of that lovely cove
Warmed with the painter's soul of love.
     Alive with summer's gorgeous hues,
     And sparkling with the morning dews.
Beneath an auction hammer sold,
     Goes up to the halls of a father proud;
And a daughter's suitor chosen for his gold
     Deigns to speak his heartless praise aloud:
"In summer THAT must surely be a nice retreat.
"The city is so tedious with its dust and heat!"

STORY OF A DEW DROP.

In a hare-bell cup, at the break of day,
Sparkling and bright a dew-drop lay.

When ruddy morn the east o'erspread,
The dew-drop caught the rays it shed,

And blending with them the floweret's blue
It rivaled the gem with its delicate hue.

But the sun, when he rose, was wroth to see
A dew-drop could shine more brightly than he:

So he sent down a beam to the hare-bell cup,
And drank the drop in its beauty up.

And such is the law in nature's plan :
Subject to it is the fate of man.

Life is the dew in the hare-bell cup,
And death the beam that shall drink it up.

Bowdoin College, April, 1859.

THE SEA.

O, ceaseless, surging Sea,
Pathless, impressionless, type of eternity!
Nor time, nor change has left a trace,
A single furrow on thy face.
The solid earth is seamed with scars,
Deep-graven records of her wars;
And tells in fissured rock and chasm
How many a fearful shock and spasm
The ancient sphere has shaken!
But thou, oh Sea,
When awful memories waken,
In solemn stillness of the night,
Canst slumber childlike in the light
Of the desolate moon and silent stars!
Hadst thou a brooding soul, oh Sea,
Then wert thou of remorse ne'er free;
Were souls remorseless half, as thou art,
How many a pang were saved and bleeding
heart!

Packet, "S. Curling," from Boston to Liverpool, September, 1861.

ON LOCH KATRINE.

With bracken brown and purple heather
Clan Alpine's ancient hills are drest,
While o'er the clouds in perfect weather
Ben Lomond lifts his airy crest.

But not a ripple stirs the tide
Of Loch Katrine, the queenly lake,
As o'er its silvery face we glide,
Save those the highland oarsmen make.

The ruined sides of Ben Venue
Are steep and rugged as of yore,
When brave Fitz-James and Roderick Dhu
Contended on yon rocky shore.

And Ellen's Isle, romantic spot,
A fit retreat for outlawed earl,
Is no less famed for Walter Scott
Than for the Douglas' lovely girl.

The autumn evening lingering low,
Now hastens, ere the sun is set,
To fling its last expiring glow
Around each rocky minaret,

That from the bristling Trosachs towers,
Suggestive of that earlier age
When fierce the grim Titanic powers
Their elemental wars did wage.

But as we near the flinty strand
Where still Loch Katrine's waters lave,
The sentry cliffs, that silent stand
And guard the Goblin's ancient cave,

Each rock and hill and mountain bold,
Beneath our feet reflected lies;
And, crowned with evening's virgin gold,
Doth dazzle our admiring eyes.

No siren sings upon the cliff,
And yet in transport must we gaze
As gazed the boatman from his skiff
To see the Lurlei's mantle blaze.

So sweet in sleep was never dream
As was our waking dream that day:
Oh, was it, pray, a bright foregleam
Of life that shall endure alway?

Stirling, Scotland, October, 1861.

TO MY COUNTRYMEN.

Strike home! ye patriot hearts, your cause is just,
    No tyrant's banners lead you to the field;
For freedom and your brave forefathers' dust,
    Will ye to knaves such blood-bought treasures
        yield?
Strike home! not for ourselves alone the fight,
    Each blow you deal clanks on oppression's chains;
For all the world, for universal right—
    Each drop is gold that flows from your free veins.

It is a fearful drama which you play,
    And anxious Europe on the issue waits;
Her *people's* hearts are with our cause to-day,
    For there are written, too, *their* future fates.
What wonder, then, her tyrants madly frown,
    When victory our starry banner spreads;
Who forge the chains to bind God's image down
    Well know the wrath that hovers o'er their heads.

America—where liberty was born,
    The North and South united as her fane—
Shall future monarchs live to tell in scorn,
    How blood and treasure shielded her in vain?
Ah! no, by all that freemen's hearts hold dear,
    Our fire-sides and the name of WASHINGTON!
Strike home! again our glorious standard rear
    O'er this proud brotherhood, forever one.

Heidelberg, Germany, May. 1862.

EVENING IN THE PAYS DE VAUD.

O'er Jura's craggy peaks aglow,
  The gorgeous sunlight lingers;
In deep crevasse 'mid Alpine snow
  It dips its rosy fingers.

Along Lake Leman's vine-girt shore
  Is mild and balmy weather,
While overhead on ledges hoar
  Eternal icebergs gather.

And where the avalanches creep
  From off the cloud-toucht mountains,
The azure Rhone, o'er rock and steep,
  Comes dashing from its fountains.

But now the ebon veil descends,
  And night enshrouds the valley,
Save where its light the glow worm lends
  In wall or trellised alley.

I hear the plover's plaintive note,
  The murmur of the billows;
And Philomel's sweet ditties float
  From out the sighing willows.

Anon sweet music fills the air
  From many a garden bower
Where rustic swains and maids repair
  To spend this charmëd hour.

How like a vision all things seem
  Beyond this vale of shadows ;
E'en as I muse, the young day's beam
  Lights up my native meadows.

And thus, alas, it is with all,
  'Tis distant and uncertain
If once or time, or space let fall
  Twixt us and it the curtain.

The home that's left, the life that's o'er,
  The friend that death has taken,
In dreamy hours return once more,
  But never if we waken.

Vevay, Switzerland. June. 1862.

IN THE CHAMPS ELYSEES.

Her blithe voice quivers through the song,
Her light foot trembles on the stage,
While the motley, gay and unkempt throng
Encore unceasing in their rage of ecstasy.
But when the curtain a third time fell,
All tremulous and pale with toil
She broke away as from a spell;
And as their plaudits rose the while, unseen
  of living eye,
In breathless haste she took her way
To where the sluggish river lay
Like a serpent, basking in the light
Of the mirky, moon deserted night.

And when she stood upon the bank
And heard the slow tide's breathing,
Her heart in hopeless sorrow sank,
And she felt herself the wasted thing
She was, whose soul's best treasure
Was squandered to the guilty pleasure
Of one who loved her not.
And as she stood beside the river
Almost motionless and ever
Emitting from its slimy breast

The odor of a noisome pest,
She sank upon the spot;
And dim before her wildered vision,
She saw the world in proud derision
In the Champs Elysées point her out:
And withered, tottering with age,
She still was singing on the stage;
But for her plaudits rose a shout
Of scorn, and she awoke again
From out that half prophetic swoon
To feel her limbs benumbed with pain,
And wish that one eternal swoon
Her blighted life might be,
The hollow, vague and far-off sounding roar
Of the river, as from some distant shore,
Beyond the bourn of this cold sphere
Called her with fascination drear,   .
And she was left no choice but follow.
And the people, the boors and rabble rout,
And gay grisettes whose merry shout
Made bright her gala night,
Go down with transient tears of sorrow
To the charnel Morgue, on the grim morrow,
To look upon their favorite.

DIRGE.

The flower was blighted in thy breath,
   O, ardent love of noon;

And dew drops moistened, it drooped in death
   Under thy light, pale moon!
   Its sweet fragrance was fled
   Like the souls of the dead ;
O, Earth, why claim'st thou thine own so
     soon !

A saintly thing is a sinless soul,—
   Suspicionless of guile;
In Notre Dame with solemn knoll
   Peals the minster bell the while ;
   With funeral knoll,
   Pray let it toll,
As the mourners move down the hollow aisle.

The world is rigid in rules of right,
   Though apt itself to wrong;
In judging the weak it takes delight.
   But bows the knee to the strong.
   Rest, lost one, rest
   In the dark grave's breast ;
Justice in giving its dues is long.

Paris. September. 1862.

STANZAS SUGGESTED BY THE WAR.

SEPTEMBER, 1864.

The nights grow longer as the weeks go by,
And now her reign begins the harvest moon;
In dreamy haze the sunlight swims by noon,
And all the distant hills seem doubly high.

The forest leaves have breathed the young frost's
      breath,
And rustle in the dreary winds of fall;
Ripe for the reaper's hand the broad fields all,—
The gray old year is hastening to its death.

The rose-cheeked apples wear a mellower tinge;
From bursting husks the golden maize ears gleam,
And in gay semblance of the spring time seem
The trees, festooned with autumn's fiery fringe.

Nay, let the earth these tawdry vestments wear,
The mournful harbingers of meet decay;
Death claims a nobler sacrifice to-day
Than crowns the altar of the dying year.

Ere long when winds have swept the brown fields
      bare,
And play strange antics with the leafless limbs,

The longed for peace will chant its matin hymns.
An empty peace whose voidness is despair.

Ah, then shall wearied nature take its rest;
The aching atoms worn with ceaseless strife
Shall quit the nerveless grasp of wasted life,
To swell the mould in earth's insensate breast.

But why complain if brief the season seem ?
This fever flush betokening decay
Is but the prelude of that better day
The earth shall waken from its wintry dream.

Thou, too, oh man, in endless toil must tire ;
The buoyant hopes of youth sink low with age ;
Worn out at length with life's turmoil and rage,
Thou'lt yield to death as stubble yields to fire.

There's little solace in the heartless vaunt
That for an end benign is war decreed,
That else in time the earth would fail to feed
Its populations vast, and come to want.

The public weal holds single lives full cheap,
And nations plethoric with plenty grown
Are soonest with the seeds of discord sown ;
The fields drink blood while maids and mothers
        weep.

In life's philosophy there's little balm
To sooth the pain the timid spirit fills;
His soul tastes joy supreme whom valor thrills:
'Tis only cravens shrink from fancied harm.

Then boom the gun, the drummer beat *reveille ;*
The screaming shot, the madly shrieking shell,
What though to myriads they sound the knell,—
While war endures, life's fount will never fail!

REST.

Oh, what is rest?
Hope long deferred, by daily promise fed,
  Doth make my spirit tire!
As years go by, I joy to see them sped.
  In eagerness of my desire
For rest, I long to lie among the quiet dead,
  Beneath the pall of green that wraps each mound
  In yonder silent burial ground!

Yet, what is rest?
That blissful rest which we so much do crave,
　And fain would find within the hollow grave?
I've watched an eagle float on moveless wing
　Beneath the zenith all one afternoon,
And glide about as 'twere an easy thing
　To wait in air and perch upon the moon.

He seemed at rest,
Yet I have somewhere heard
　That only unremitting toil could stay
The pinions of the bird,
　And keep him safe upon his dizzy way;
And that 'twas when he most did seem at rest,
That every sinew of his noble breast
　Was strained to all its utmost strength would
　　bear,
　To buoy him upward on the yielding air.

Still, what is rest?
Why further strive, a simple truth to learn,
　When all the earth doth the same lesson teach?
Wilt thou unto the elements but turn,
　They will admonish thee, though 'reft of speech,
That rest, the same for which thy soul doth yearn,
　Is found where strength and will harmonious
　　blend,
　And work together for a common end.

OUR DEAD.

Memorial Sonnets read at the Triennial Meeting of the Class of 1861, Bowdoin College, August, 1864.

NELSON PERLEY CRAM.

Soft be his sleep beneath the waving pines,
And zephyrs hush his wearied soul to rest;
Sweet is their wail that whispers he is blest,
Freed from the strife at which this life repines.

Locked in the future's lap are its designs
For all who venture its uncertain wave;
Who bravely meets its certain goal, the grave,—
Around his brow the crown of valor shines.

He's paid the debt of all of mother born,
Gone in the promise of his life's young morn,
To join the throng whose earthly work is done.

Fresh as the flowers that deck his early tomb,
In our sad hearts his memory shall bloom,
Till like his own our mortal race is run.

SAMUEL FESSENDEN.

Ah! speechless soul where deepest sinks regret,
The heart that feels is quietest in grief;
Nor in bland words would craven find relief,
But loves the woe it can ne'er more forget.

So in our hearts is silent sorrow yet,
Nor words essay its burden to relieve;
With arid eyes and stoic lips we grieve
Beside the grave we have not tears to wet.

Three years ago we stood together side
By side, and now he's sleeping by the sea;
It ebbs and flows, its ceaseless, careless tide.

Ne'er manhood graced a manlier form,
A dearer friend ne'er walked the earth than he.
Alas! the young oak's blasted by the storm.

JOHN RICH.

The great, unfeeling world, with crash and din,
Moves down the tide of swift revolving years:
Around the vortex of to-day careers,
The next forgets that yesterday has been.

Intent on that they've set their hearts to win,
Men blindly dash toward the goal of gain ;
Nor know, nor feel they for a brother's pain,
But hush the sympathy that pleads within.

To make our marks upon the shifting sands
We came with aspirations fixed and high ;
Intent on lifting self were brain and hands.

He walked beside us there, but ne'er bespoke
Amid his hopes and fears our sympathy,
And we ne'er knew his heart until it broke.

WILLIAM WILSON MORRELL.

And sealed in death are those dear lips for aye
Which pleaded for us at the throne of grace ;
What heavenly trust lit up his manly face
Upon that last, that gone reunion day !

We all declared 'twas good to hear him pray ;
Bold in his words stood out the soul sincere ;
In awe we bowed and owned God's presence
          near,
E'en though unused to walk in Godly way.

Alas ! what changes bring the fickle years ;
He rests in peace upon that gory field
Still quaking with a nation's hopes and fears.

Farewell thou valiant heart, thy work is done ;
The sword of right, the mightiest thou didst
          wield,—
The meed all just, the hero's grave thou'st won.

TRANSLATIONS.

DOWN YONDER IN THE MILL.

[FROM THE GERMAN OF JUSTINUS KERNER.]

Down yonder in the mill
  In sweet repose I lay,
And saw the wheel go round,
  And saw the waters play:

Beheld the saw so bright;
  To me 'twas like a dream,
As in the fir-tree's trunk
  It cut its narrow seam.

The fir it seemed to live:
  And, to the saw's rough stroke,
While all its fibres rung,
  These were the words it spoke:

"Thou com'st in goodly time,
  O wanderer, in here;
Thou art for whom the wound
  My heart hath pressed so near.

"Thou art for whom shall be,
  When short thou'st wandered here,
This wood in earth's cold lap
  An everlasting bier."

Four boards! I saw them fall:
  My soul grew heavy then:
A word I fain had said,—
  The wheel turned ne'er again!

THE LORELEY.*

[FROM THE GERMAN OF HEINE.]

I know not what the cause may be
   Such heaviness hath wrought,—
A legend of the olden time
   That never goes from thought ;
The air is chill, and it darkens,
   In quiet flows the Rhine,
And the mountain top, it sparkles
   In evening's gold sunshine.

The beauteous lady is seated
   Yonder, so wondrous fair ;
Her golden mantle glitters,
   She combs her golden hair ;
She combs it with golden comb,
   And a wondrous ditty sings :
With echoing of her melody,
   Each cliff and valley rings.

The boatman in his tiny craft,
   Is seized with wildest woe ;
Entranced he only looks on high,
   Nor sees the frowning rocks below.
I believe the waves, at last,
   The heedless man will drown.
And this, with her sweet singing,
   The Loreley has done !

---

*Pronounced *Loraly.*

SONG OF THE YOUNG MOUNTAINEER.

[FROM THE GERMAN OF UHLAND.]

I am the mountain shepherd boy,
The castles all below me lie ;
The morning sun beams first up here,
And longest too the day is near ;
O, I'm the youthful mountaineer.

'Tis here the river has its birth,
I drink it fresh from stone and earth ;
It roars from cliff with wild alarms,
I clasp it here in my two arms ;
O, I'm the youthful mountaineer.

The mountain is my proper sphere,
The storms they rage about me here ;
From north and south the tempests spring,
Above them rise the songs I sing ;
O, I'm the youthful mountaineer.

Are lightnings darting under me,
Here in clear air their sport I see ;
I know them well, and thus I cry ;
My father's house in peace pass by ;
O, I'm the youthful mountaineer.

And when alarm-bells once may sound,
And watch-fires glow on mountains round,
I go below, I join the throng,
And swing my sword and sing my song ;
O, I'm the youthful mountaineer.

THE RESOLVE.

[PARAPHRASED FROM UHLAND.]

She's coming through the quiet glade :—
To-day I'll loose my timid tongue ;
Why should I fear before the maid
Whom, for my life, I would not wrong?

To greet her, all so ready are !
But I, poor fool, pass sheepish by ;
And to my heaven's cherished star
Have not yet dared to lift an eye.

The flowers that bloom about her feet,
The birds with carols soft and sweet,
All dare for her their love confess ;
Then surely I should do no less.

I'll lay me down by yonder stream,
Where oft the maiden passes by,
And talk, as 'twere, in dulcet dream,
Of her I love, unconsciously.

I will—ah, woe is me, what fright !
There, there she comes ! where shall I fly !
Behind this tree I'm out of sight,—
She heeds me not, but passes by.

A REMINISCENCE.

From out the dim, almost forgotten past,
One scene, unbid, will oft to mind recur;
How fondly in affection's shrine they last,—
The sad, sweet memories of the things that were!

It was the quiet of a Sabbath day,
And lonesome grass-fields nodded in the breeze:
The spreading farms in summer sunshine lay,
And vests of verdure clothed the forest trees.

The tired cattle sought the thicket's shade;
The woodland rill went rippling on its way,—
While feathered songsters warbled in the glade,
And silent swallows chased their insect prey.

A motley throng stand round the farm-house door,
Or move about with slow and cautious tread;
Young men and boys, and sires whose heads are
        hoar,
Have met in tearful tribute to the dead.

When erst the roses in the warm May air
Put forth their tender blossoms to the light,
The fairest flower that bloomed would ill compare
With her who lieth now in death-shroud white.

The red-rose tint was on her cheek so fair,
Her dark eyes tender as the dewy morn,—
While night itself was mirrored in the hair
She chose the timid snow-drop to adorn.

The mother's idol and the father's pride,
The reigning queen of each successive May,
Her sovereignty by rival ne'er denied,—
She ruled her realm of love with easy sway.

What wonder then that gallants, by the score,
On bended knee for heart and hand should sue?
Both young and old such charms might well adore;
Who loved her not her graces never knew.

But death delights with choicest flowers to fill
His cypress wreath to crown the circling years;
And vain to stay his hand is human skill,
Or prayers, or threats, or mourners' bitter tears.

* * * * * * * *

The funeral rites were simple, brief and sad;
Too young the preacher's words to recollect,
I've learned that for the friends good cheer he had;
Though most abused, his was no gloomy sect.

But not of dogmas dry would I discourse,
In this my simple retrospective lay,

But turn again to view the sable hearse
As down the lane it slowly takes its way.

Beside the grave the dumb procession stands,
And weeping mourners take their last farewell :
The stricken mother wrings her aged hands,
And tears are vain her agony to tell.

Well might'st thou weep, could weeping life re-
      store!
But nought shall rend from death the envied prize :
That silvery voice shall greet thine ear no more,
No more on thine shall beam those beauteous eyes!

The coffin sinks in the relentless ground,
That shall restore its precious gift no more ;
The falling earth sends up a muffled sound,
The grave is closed, and with it all is o'er!

Ah no, not o'er! exclaim all reasoning men,
With emphasis that sounds the centuries through,
Except some timid spirits, now and then,
Who doubt if life itself is really true.

Death is not Lord! where heaven's best gifts are
      lost,
Is here in this frail life we live below ;
Ah, fortunate, whom cares have tempest-tost,
Possessing all unsullied, hence may go.

If souls are pure, 'tis only flesh can die ;
And grace and beauty thrown about us here,
Are seamless mantles, from the wardrobe high,
To deck the soul for its celestial sphere.

Then let us not forget, as oft we turn
The lingering memories of the past to con,
That still the dead, for whom our spirits yearn,
In ways that win us most, are living on.